12-Month Journal

MY MONTHLY JOURNAL
JANUARY 20___

DAY 1

DAY 2

DAY 3

DAY 4

DAY 5

DAY 6

DAY 7

I WILL PROGRESS BY:

I WILL PROGRESS BY:

...FROM THIS MOMENT FORWARD!

...FROM THIS MOMENT FORWARD!

MY MONTHLY JOURNAL

DAY 8

DAY 9

DAY 10

DAY 11

DAY 12

DAY 13

DAY 14

DAY 15

DAY 16

I WILL PROGRESS BY:

...FROM THIS MOMENT FORWARD!

...FROM THIS MOMENT FORWARD!

MY MONTHLY JOURNAL

DAY 17

DAY 18

DAY 19

DAY 20

DAY 21

DAY 22

DAY 23

DAY 24

I WILL PROGRESS BY:

I WILL PROGRESS BY:

...FROM THIS MOMENT FORWARD!

...FROM THIS MOMENT FORWARD!

MY MONTHLY JOURNAL

DAY 25 _____

DAY 26 _____

DAY 27 _____

DAY 28 _____

DAY 29 _____

DAY 30 _____

DAY 31 _____

- -

Congratulations!

You've Made it Through This Month By Finding
Peace Within Yourself.

NOTES. NOTES. NOTES. NOTES. NOTES. NOTES.

MY MONTHLY JOURNAL
FEBRUARY 20___

Forever Lotus

MY AFFIRMATIONS:
I am a Great Mother.
I will be kind to my kids today.
My children light up my life.

DAY 1 _____

DAY 2 _____

DAY 3 _____

DAY 4 _____

DAY 5 _____

DAY 6 _____

DAY 7 _____

I WILL PROGRESS BY:

...FROM THIS MOMENT FORWARD!

MY MONTHLY
JOURNAL

DAY 8
_____

DAY 9
_____

DAY 10
_____

DAY 11
_____

DAY 12
_____

DAY 13
_____

DAY 14
_____

DAY 15
_____

DAY 16
_____

I WILL PROGRESS BY:

...FROM THIS MOMENT FORWARD!

MY MONTHLY JOURNAL

DAY 17

DAY 18

DAY 19

DAY 20

DAY 21

DAY 22

DAY 23

DAY 24

I WILL PROGRESS BY:

...FROM THIS MOMENT FORWARD!

MY MONTHLY JOURNAL

DAY 25
_____
_____

DAY 26
_____
_____

DAY 27
_____
_____

DAY 28
_____
_____

DAY 29
_____
_____
_____
_____
_____

Congratulations!

You Found Joy in Ways You Wouldn't Have
Imagined by Staying Positive.

GET THE DETAILS...

MY MONTHLY JOURNAL
MARCH 20____

MY AFFIRMATIONS:

Parenting is a journey; I will trust where God is leading me.
God is guiding me today. I can hear his voice clearly.
I am training my children in the right way.

DAY 1 _____

DAY 2 _____

DAY 3 _____

DAY 4 _____

DAY 5 _____

DAY 6 _____

DAY 7 _____

I WILL PROGRESS BY:

...FROM THIS MOMENT FORWARD!

MY MONTHLY JOURNAL

Forever Lotus

DAY 8

DAY 9

DAY 10

DAY 11

DAY 12

DAY 13

DAY 14

DAY 15

DAY 16

I WILL PROGRESS BY:

...FROM THIS MOMENT FORWARD!

MY MONTHLY JOURNAL

DAY 17

DAY 18

DAY 19

DAY 20

DAY 21

DAY 22

DAY 23

DAY 24

I WILL PROGRESS BY:

...FROM THIS MOMENT FORWARD!

MY MONTHLY JOURNAL

DAY 25

DAY 26

DAY 27

DAY 28

DAY 29

DAY 30

DAY 31

Congratulations!

Your Journey Has Been Planned Out Thanks to Your Listening Ear.

GET THE DETAILS...

NOTES. NOTES. NOTES. NOTES. NOTES. NOTES.

MY MONTHLY JOURNAL
APRIL 20____

MY AFFIRMATIONS:
I love my children.
I love myself.
I am doing my best.

DAY 1

DAY 2

DAY 3

DAY 4

DAY 5

DAY 6

DAY 7

I WILL PROGRESS BY:

...FROM THIS MOMENT FORWARD!

MY MONTHLY
JOURNAL

DAY 8

_____

DAY 9

_____

DAY 10

_____

DAY 11

_____

DAY 12

_____

DAY 13

_____

DAY 14

_____

 DAY 15

_____

DAY 16

_____

I WILL PROGRESS BY:

...FROM THIS MOMENT FORWARD!

MY MONTHLY JOURNAL

DAY 17

DAY 18

DAY 19

DAY 20

DAY 21

DAY 22

DAY 23

DAY 24

I WILL PROGRESS BY:

...FROM THIS MOMENT FORWARD!

DAY 25

DAY 26

DAY 27

DAY 28

DAY 29

DAY 30

Congratulations!

You Found Self-Love and Can Now Love Others Fully.

GET THE DETAILS...

NOTES. NOTES. NOTES. NOTES. NOTES. NOTES.

MY MONTHLY JOURNAL
MAY 20____

DAY 1 _____

DAY 2 _____

DAY 3 _____

DAY 4 _____

DAY 5 _____

DAY 6 _____

DAY 7 _____

I WILL PROGRESS BY:

...FROM THIS MOMENT FORWARD!

MY MONTHLY JOURNAL

DAY 8
_____

DAY 9
_____

DAY 10
_____

DAY 11
_____

DAY 12
_____

DAY 13
_____

DAY 14
_____

DAY 15
_____

DAY 16
_____

I WILL PROGRESS BY:

...FROM THIS MOMENT FORWARD!

MY MONTHLY JOURNAL

DAY 17

DAY 18

DAY 19

DAY 20

DAY 21

DAY 22

DAY 23

DAY 24

I WILL PROGRESS BY:

...FROM THIS MOMENT FORWARD!

MY MONTHLY JOURNAL

DAY 25
_____

DAY 26
_____

DAY 27
_____

DAY 28
_____

DAY 29
_____

DAY 30
_____

DAY 31
_____

- -

Congratulations!

You Remembered to Give Yourself Grace to Complete Tasks.

NOTES. NOTES. NOTES. NOTES. NOTES. NOTES.

MY MONTHLY JOURNAL
JUNE 20 _____

Forever Lotus

MY AFFIRMATIONS:
Being a mother has shown me how strong I am.
Every challenge that I face makes me a better mom.
God gave me these kids. He will give me the strength to provide for them.

DAY 1 _____

_____

DAY 2 _____

_____

DAY 3 _____

_____

DAY 4 _____

_____

DAY 5 _____

_____

DAY 6 _____

_____

DAY 7 _____

_____

I WILL PROGRESS BY:

...FROM THIS MOMENT FORWARD!

MY MONTHLY JOURNAL

Forever Lotus

DAY 8
_____

DAY 9
_____

DAY 10
_____

DAY 11
_____

DAY 12
_____

DAY 13
_____

DAY 14
_____

DAY 15
_____

DAY 16
_____

I WILL PROGRESS BY:

...FROM THIS MOMENT FORWARD!

MY MONTHLY JOURNAL

Forever Lotus

DAY 17

DAY 18

DAY 19

DAY 20

DAY 21

DAY 22

DAY 23

DAY 24

I WILL PROGRESS BY:

...FROM THIS MOMENT FORWARD!

DAY 25

DAY 26

DAY 27

DAY 28

DAY 29

DAY 30

Congratulations!

You Have Found Your Strength Through Your
Greatest Gift: Motherhood.

GET THE DETAILS...

NOTES. NOTES. NOTES. NOTES. NOTES. NOTES.

MY MONTHLY JOURNAL
JULY 20____

MY AFFIRMATIONS:
God will grant me understanding and patience when it comes to what my child needs.
No one understands my child like me.
I understand that I can not always be with my child but when I am not God is there.

DAY 1

DAY 2

DAY 3

DAY 4

DAY 5

DAY 6

DAY 7

I WILL PROGRESS BY:

...FROM THIS MOMENT FORWARD!

MY MONTHLY JOURNAL

Forever Lotus

DAY 8

DAY 9

DAY 10

DAY 11

DAY 12

DAY 13

DAY 14

DAY 15

DAY 16

I WILL PROGRESS BY:

...FROM THIS MOMENT FORWARD!

MY MONTHLY JOURNAL

DAY 17

DAY 18

DAY 19

DAY 20

DAY 21

DAY 22

DAY 23

DAY 24

I WILL PROGRESS BY:

...FROM THIS MOMENT FORWARD!

MY MONTHLY JOURNAL

ForeverLotus

DAY 25

DAY 26

DAY 27

DAY 28

DAY 29

DAY 30

DAY 31

Congratulations!
You Understand and Can Better
Guide the Little Mind(s) Your Body Created.

NOTES. NOTES. NOTES. NOTES. NOTES. NOTES.

MY MONTHLY JOURNAL
AUGUST 20____

MY AFFIRMATIONS:
I am a Great Mom because I love my kids.
I am making the best decisions for my family.
It's ok to have a bad moment, however it will only be a moment. My kids need me.

DAY 1

DAY 2

DAY 3

DAY 4

DAY 5

DAY 6

DAY 7

I WILL PROGRESS BY:

...FROM THIS MOMENT FORWARD!

MY MONTHLY
JOURNAL

DAY 8

DAY 9

DAY 10

DAY 11

DAY 12

DAY 13

DAY 14

DAY 15

DAY 16

I WILL PROGRESS BY:

I WILL PROGRESS BY:

...FROM THIS MOMENT FORWARD!

...FROM THIS MOMENT FORWARD!

MY MONTHLY JOURNAL

DAY 17

DAY 18

DAY 19

DAY 20

DAY 21

DAY 22

DAY 23

DAY 24

I WILL PROGRESS BY:

...FROM THIS MOMENT FORWARD!

...FROM THIS MOMENT FORWARD!

DAY 25

DAY 26

DAY 27

DAY 28

DAY 29

DAY 30

DAY 31

Congratulations!

You Found Patience Through Prayer and
Meditation to Be at Your Best.

NOTES. NOTES. NOTES. NOTES. NOTES. NOTES.

GET THE DETAILS...

NOTES. NOTES. NOTES. NOTES. NOTES. NOTES.

MY MONTHLY
JOURNAL
SEPTEMBER 20____

MY AFFIRMATIONS:
With God's Wisdom, I am guiding my children into a great life.
I will seek God for wisdom on how to be the best mother daily.
God will give me the wisdom I need to be a great mom.

DAY 1
_____
_____

DAY 2
_____
_____

DAY 3
_____
_____

DAY 4
_____
_____

DAY 5
_____
_____

DAY 6
_____
_____

DAY 7
_____
_____

I WILL PROGRESS BY:

...FROM THIS MOMENT FORWARD!

MY MONTHLY JOURNAL

DAY 8

DAY 9

DAY 10

DAY 11

DAY 12

DAY 13

DAY 14

DAY 15

DAY 16

I WILL PROGRESS BY:

...FROM THIS MOMENT FORWARD!

MY MONTHLY JOURNAL

Forever Lotus

DAY 17

DAY 18

DAY 19

DAY 20

DAY 21

DAY 22

DAY 23

DAY 24

I WILL PROGRESS BY:

...FROM THIS MOMENT FORWARD!

DAY 25

_____
_____

DAY 26

_____
_____

DAY 27

_____
_____

DAY 28

_____
_____

DAY 29

_____
_____

DAY 30

_____
_____
_____

Congratulations!

Your New Found Wisdom Has Provided
You the Vision of Your Child's Growth.

NOTES. NOTES. NOTES. NOTES. NOTES. NOTES.

GET THE DETAILS...

NOTES. NOTES. NOTES. NOTES. NOTES. NOTES.

MY MONTHLY JOURNAL
OCTOBER 20 _____

MY AFFIRMATIONS:
I have everything I need to be a great mom.
I am a STRONG Mama!
My God is the source of my Strength.

DAY 1

DAY 2

DAY 3

DAY 4

DAY 5

DAY 6

DAY 7

I WILL PROGRESS BY:

I WILL PROGRESS BY:

...FROM THIS MOMENT FORWARD!

...FROM THIS MOMENT FORWARD!

MY MONTHLY
JOURNAL

DAY 8
_____

DAY 9
_____

DAY 10
_____

DAY 11
_____

DAY 12
_____

DAY 13
_____

DAY 14
_____

DAY 15
_____

DAY 16
_____

I WILL PROGRESS BY:

...FROM THIS MOMENT FORWARD!

MY MONTHLY JOURNAL

DAY 17

DAY 18

DAY 19

DAY 20

DAY 21

DAY 22

DAY 23

DAY 24

I WILL PROGRESS BY:

...FROM THIS MOMENT FORWARD!

...FROM THIS MOMENT FORWARD!

MY MONTHLY JOURNAL

Forever Lotus

DAY 25

DAY 26

DAY 27

DAY 28

DAY 29

DAY 30

DAY 31

Congratulations!

Your Bravery Has Pushed You Through Another Month.

NOTES. NOTES. NOTES. NOTES. NOTES. NOTES.

MY MONTHLY JOURNAL
NOVEMBER 20____

DAY 1
_____

DAY 2
_____

DAY 3
_____

DAY 4
_____

DAY 5
_____

DAY 6
_____

DAY 7
_____

I WILL PROGRESS BY:

...FROM THIS MOMENT FORWARD!

MY MONTHLY JOURNAL

DAY 8

DAY 9

DAY 10

DAY 11

DAY 12

DAY 13

DAY 14

DAY 15

DAY 16

I WILL PROGRESS BY:

...FROM THIS MOMENT FORWARD!

MY MONTHLY JOURNAL

Forever Lotus

DAY 17

DAY 18

DAY 19

DAY 20

DAY 21

DAY 22

DAY 23

DAY 24

I WILL PROGRESS BY:

...FROM THIS MOMENT FORWARD!

DAY 25

DAY 26

DAY 27

DAY 28

DAY 29

DAY 30

Congratulations!

Your Will Power to Succeed Has Now Laid the
Foundations for Your Children to Make A Difference.

NOTES. NOTES. NOTES. NOTES. NOTES. NOTES.

NOTES. NOTES. NOTES. NOTES. NOTES. NOTES.

MY MONTHLY JOURNAL
DECEMBER 20____

MY AFFIRMATIONS:
I have God with me. I cannot fail.
I will be bold and courageous God upholds me.
From my courage my children will thrive.

DAY 1

DAY 2

DAY 3

DAY 4

DAY 5

DAY 6

DAY 7

I WILL PROGRESS BY:

...FROM THIS MOMENT FORWARD!

MY MONTHLY JOURNAL

DAY 8

DAY 9

DAY 10

DAY 11

DAY 12

DAY 13

DAY 14

DAY 15

DAY 16

I WILL PROGRESS BY:

...FROM THIS MOMENT FORWARD!

MY MONTHLY JOURNAL

Forever Lotus

DAY 17

DAY 18

DAY 19

DAY 20

DAY 21

DAY 22

DAY 23

DAY 24

I WILL PROGRESS BY:

...FROM THIS MOMENT FORWARD!

...FROM THIS MOMENT FORWARD!

MY MONTHLY JOURNAL

DAY 25 _____

DAY 26 _____

DAY 27 _____

DAY 28 _____

DAY 29 _____

DAY 30 _____

DAY 31 _____

- -

Congratulations!
You Have Found Courage to Always
Know Your Best Is Enough.

NOTES. NOTES. NOTES. NOTES. NOTES. NOTES.

Made in the USA
Coppell, TX
05 May 2022